D0538701

CALGARY PUBLIC LIBRARY

OCT 2009

For good dogs everywhere,
especially Tuna, Louise, and Sue Bee

Copyright © 2009 by Cece Bell

All rights reserved. No part of this book may be reproduced,
transmitted, or stored in an information retrieval system in any form
or by any means, graphic, electronic, or mechanical, including
photocopying, taping, and recording, without prior
written permission from the publisher.

First edition 2009

Library of Congress Cataloging-in-Publication Data is available.
Library of Congress Catalog Card Number 2008929145
ISBN 978-0-7636-3616-6

2 4 6 8 10 9 7 5 3 1

Printed in China

This book was typeset in Joe Overweight.
The illustrations were done in acrylic with ink.

Candlewick Press
99 Dover Street
Somerville, Massachusetts 02144

visit us at www.candlewick.com

ITTY BITTY

Cece Bell

CANDLEWICK PRESS

Itty Bitty is a dog.
A very, very tiny dog.

One day, Itty Bitty found a bone.
A very, very enormous bone.

This bone is big enough to be my home, thought Itty Bitty.

Itty Bitty quickly got to work.

He chewed a hole
in the middle of the
bone . . .

and a hole on
either side.

He chewed and chewed until the bone was completely hollow inside.

Satisfactory!

Itty Bitty's work was done.

But the bone didn't quite feel
like home.

I need some itty-bitty things to put inside my home, thought Itty Bitty.

I'm going shopping!

E DEE DEPAR

Itty Bitty pulled up to a great big
department store and went inside.

Just as Itty Bitty began to worry
that he wouldn't find anything in
his size, he saw a little sign.

BUT WAIT—
there's more!
This way!

He found an itty-bitty table and
an itty-bitty rug . . .

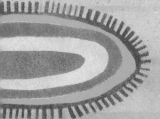

an itty-bitty sofa,

and an itty-bitty lamp.

He even found an itty-bitty book.

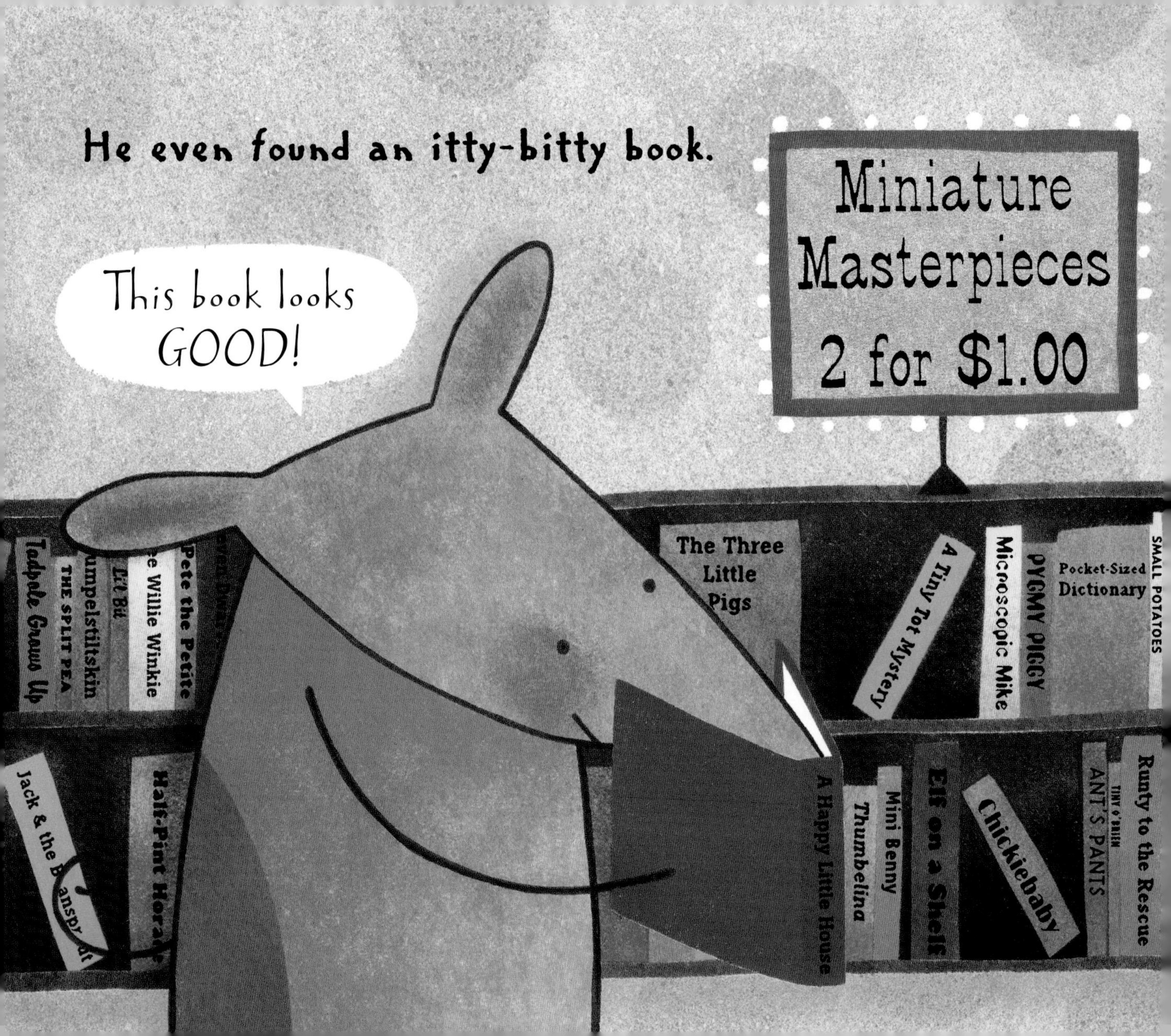

Itty Bitty bought everything he liked and
brought it back to the enormous bone.

Then Itty Bitty put everything inside.

It felt like home.